Our Emotions and Behavior

I Don't Want to Be Nice!

Sue Graves

Illustrated by Emanuela Carletti and Desideria Guicciardini

free spirit
PUBLISHING®

Finn was in Mr. Hare's class.
Finn was **not very kind**.
He cared mostly about himself.
He didn't help when Ahmed felt sick.

He didn't help Lily reach her coat.

At recess, everyone played soccer.
But Finn **didn't play fair.**
He knocked Freddy over.

He pushed Molly out of the way.

3

Molly said Finn was **not nice.**
She said he should play fair.

But Finn didn't want to play fair.
He said being nice was boring!

5

Everyone was **mad** at Finn.
They told Mr. Hare about it.
Mr. Hare had a good idea.

Mr. Hare said Finn would be Jake's **buddy**. Jake was new at school. Mr. Hare said Finn should spend the day with Jake and **help him**.

But Finn **didn't want** to be Jake's buddy. He didn't spend time with him at all. He didn't help him hang up his coat.

10

Finn didn't show Jake around the school. Jake got lost. He was **very upset**.

Molly told Finn that Jake had a bad start at school because of him. She said Finn was **not nice.**

Finn did **not feel happy.**

At recess, no one played with Finn.
They said he was **too mean**.
They said he didn't play fair.
Finn was **sad**.
Mr. Hare had a talk with him.

Mr. Hare said that if Finn wanted friends, he needed to **play fair** and **be nice** to people. He said Finn should try to **make things right.**

Finn thought about it.

He said he would tell everyone he was **sorry for being unkind.**

He said he would **help** Jake.

He said he would try to play fair, too.

Mr. Hare said those were all good ideas.

Finn told everyone he was **Sorry**.

He helped Jake hang up his coat.

He showed him around the school.

17

At recess, everyone played basketball. Finn was **very kind**. He gave Molly his gloves to keep her warm.

He helped Jake score a point.
He **played fair**, too.

Jake said Finn was the **best buddy** ever! Finn decided he liked being a buddy.

He liked playing fair, too.

Being nice wasn't boring at all!

Can you tell the story of what happens when Amy and Henry decorate their pots?

How do you think Henry felt when Amy grabbed
the paint? How does he feel at the end?

A note about sharing this book

The **Our Emotions and Behavior** series has been developed to provide a starting point for further discussion about children's feelings and behavior, in relation both to themselves and to other people.

I Don't Want to Be Nice!
This story looks at the importance of playing considerately with other children. It points out the importance of being aware of others' needs and being prepared to help rather than ignore others' difficulties.

Picture story
The picture story on pages 22 and 23 provides an opportunity for speaking and listening. Children are encouraged to tell the story illustrated in the panels: Henry and Amy are painting their pots until Amy snatches the green paint from Henry, spilling it on the table. Henry is upset that he cannot finish his pot, and a classmate comes to his rescue, scolding Amy for grabbing the paint. Amy feels bad for upsetting Henry. Finally, the three classmates finish decorating their pots together.

How to use the book
The book is designed for adults to share with either an individual child or a group of children, and as a starting point for discussion.

The book also provides visual support and repeated words and phrases to build confidence in children who are starting to read on their own.

Before reading the story
Choose a time to read when you and the children are relaxed and have time to share the story.

Spend time looking at the illustrations and discussing what the book may be about before reading it together.

After reading, talk about the book with the children

- What was the story about? Have the children ever felt angry or upset because someone did not play nicely and perhaps spoiled a game?

- Have they ever been mean to others? Invite children to relate their experiences. How did the other children respond to them? How did they make things right?

- Has anyone been inconsiderate or unkind to them at school or during a game? How did they feel? What did they do about it? Did someone, such as a teacher or an older child, help them resolve the problem? How?

- Ask the children to talk about the importance of playing fair. How does it improve a game? Point out that not playing nicely can spoil a game for others and also for themselves.

To Isabelle, William A., George, William G., Max, Emily, Leo, Caspar, Felix, and Phoebe—S.G.

Published in North America by Free Spirit Publishing Inc., Minneapolis, Minnesota, 2017

Library of Congress Cataloging-in-Publication Data
Names: Graves, Sue, 1950– author. | Carletti, Emanuela, illustrator. | Guicciardini, Desideria, illustrator.
Title: I don't want to be nice! / Sue Graves ; illustrated by Emanuela Carletti and Desideria Guicciardini.
Description: Minneapolis : Free Spirit Publishing Inc., 2017. | Series: Our emotions and behavior
Identifiers: LCCN 2016033764 | ISBN 9781631981326 (hardcover) | ISBN 1631981323 (hardcover)
Subjects: LCSH: Interpersonal relations in children—Juvenile literature. | Kindness—Juvenile literature. | Children—
    Conduct of life—Juvenile literature.
Classification: LCC BF723.I646 G73 2017 | DDC 177/.7—dc23
LC record available at https://lccn.loc.gov/2016033764

Reading Level Grade 1; Interest Level Ages 4–8 ; Fountas & Pinnell Guided Reading Level I

10 9 8 7 6 5 4 3 2 1
Printed in China
S14101016

Free Spirit Publishing Inc.
6325 Sandburg Road, Suite 100
Minneapolis, MN 55427-3674
(612) 338-2068
help4kids@freespirit.com
www.freespirit.com

First published in 2017 by Franklin Watts, a division of Hachette Children's Books · London, UK, and Sydney, Australia

Text © Franklin Watts 2017
Illustrations © Emanuela Carletti and Desideria Guicciardini 2017

The rights of Sue Graves to be identified as the author and Emanuela Carletti and Desideria Guicciardini as the illustrators of this Work have been asserted in accordance with the Copyright, Designs and Patents Act, 1988.

Editor: Jackie Hamley
Designer: Peter Scoulding